The A to Z

Sports Joke Book

From **Archery** to **Zip-Lining**!

Illustrated by Vasco Icuza

Kane Miller
A DIVISION OF EDC PUBLISHING

The A to Z Sports Joke Book

If you are a sports lover with a great sense of humor, then you'll get a big kick out of this book!

The A to Z Sports Joke Book is a knee-slapping collection of over 300 sports-themed one-liners. The jokes are ordered alphabetically, so you can chuckle your way from A to Z, or search for a joke about your favorite sport. From absurd athletes to zany zip-liners, the laughs don't stop!

The A to Z Sports Joke Book is all you need to hit joke telling out of the park!

A

Q What did one **ABSEILER** say to the other?

A "I think I'm coming down with something!"

Q What do **ACROBATS**, gymnasts and bananas have in common?

A They can all do the splits!

Q What do you call an **AEROBATIC** plane that can't do tricks?

A An error-plane!

Q Why were the **AEROBICS** instructors fired?

A They didn't know squat!

Q Have you heard about the **AIKIDO** champions who enlisted?

A The first time they saluted, they nearly killed themselves!

CHORTLE!

Q What music do **ANGLERS** listen to while fishing?

A Anything catchy!

Q Why wasn't the stoplight allowed to join the **AQUATICS** team?

A Because it took too long to change!

Q What is it called when two **ARCHERS** score the same?

A A bow-tie!

Q Why can **ARCHERY** be frustrating?

A Because there are so many draw-backs!

HAHAHA!

Q Why did the **ARM WRESTLER** strap a dictionary to each arm?

A To give her biceps definition!

A

Q Why are sheep so good at **ARTISTIC GYMNASTICS**?

A They excel on uneven baaas!

Q If **ATHLETES** get athlete's foot,
what do astronauts get?

A Missile-toe!

Q Why do vegetarians boycott **ATHLETICS** competitions?

A They don't like meets!

Q What stopped the dinosaur from winning the **AUTOCROSS** race?

A A flat tire-annosaurus!

Q Did you hear about the magicians who took up
AUTOMOBILE RACING?

A They turned their cars into driveways!

Q Why was the swimmer doing the **BACKSTROKE**?

A Because he had just eaten and didn't want to swim on a full stomach!

Q What did the **BADMINTON** player say when someone shouted?

A "Who's making that racquet?!"

Q What is the only **BALL** you can see through?

A Your eyeball!

LOL!

Q Why did the **BALLET DANCER** quit?

A She found the work tutu hard!

Q Why don't dogs make good **BALLROOM DANCERS**?

A They have two left feet!

B

Q Why are spiders good **BASEBALL** players?

A They know how to catch flies!

Q What runs around a **BASEBALL FIELD** but never moves?

A The fence!

Q What did one **BASEBALL GLOVE** say to the other?

A "Catch you later!"

CACKLE!

Q Which **BASEBALL PLAYER** is full of liquid?

A The pitcher!

Q How far is it from one **BASKETBALL COURT** to the next?

A Just a hoop, skip and a jump!

Q Why do **BASKETBALL PLAYERS** love doughnuts?

A Because they can dunk them!

Q Which cricket **BATSMAN** always wears black?

A The Wicket Witch of the West!

HAHAHA!

Q Why are **BEACH VOLLEYBALL** players so good with computers?

A They are always on the net!

Q When did the **BICYCLE** get a flat tire?

A When it hit a fork in the road!

Q How do you make a ghost-proof **BICYCLE WHEEL**?

A Make sure there are no spook-es!

B

Q What do karate **BLACK BELTS** drink at parties?

A Reverse punch!

Q What does a **BMX** call its dad?

A Pop-cycle!

GIGGLE!

Q How do ducks support their **BOBSLED** team?

A They egg them on!

Q What did the ocean say to the **BODYBOARDER**?

A "Have a swell time!"

Q What happened when the dairy farmers took up **BODYBUILDING**?

A They got impressive calves!

Q What do you call a **BOOMERANG** that doesn't return?

A A stick!

Q When should **BOWLERS** wear armor?

A At knight games!

Q How quiet is a **BOWLING ALLEY**?

A So quiet you can hear a pin drop!

Q What did the **BOWLING BALL** say to the bowling pins?

A "Don't stop me, I'm on a roll!"

Q Why do **BOWLING CHAMPIONS** make bad baseball players?

A They get too many strikes!

HA HA!

Q What makes **BOWS** so accurate?

A Arrow-dynamics!

HAH!

Q When do **BOXERS** start wearing gloves?

A When it gets cold!

Q What did the comedian look for in the **BOXING RING**?

A A punchline!

Q What do archers get when they hit **BULL'S-EYES**?

A Very angry bulls!

Q What do you get when a cow goes **BUNGEE JUMPING**?

A A milkshake!

C

Q What did one **CANOE** say to the other canoe?

A "Canoe come over and play?"

Q Did you hear about the sporting goods store that had a sale on **CANOES**?

A It was quite an oar-deal!

Q Where does the baseball **CATCHER** sit at dinnertime?

A Behind the plate!

Q What did the baseball say to the catcher's glove when it was **CAUGHT**?

A "Ah, we mitt again!"

Q Why was the **CHAMPION** runner so unusual?

A Because his feet smelled while his nose ran!

HE HE!

13

C

Q What was the result of the pen versus pencil **CHAMPIONSHIP** match?

A It was a draw!

Q What is a **CHEERLEADER'S** favorite color?

A Yeller!

Q Why was the ghost on the **CHEERLEADING** squad?

A To add some team spirit!

Q How many **CLASSICAL DANCERS** does it take to change a light bulb?

A One...two...three. One...two...three!

Q What shoes do frogs wear when **CLIFF DIVING**?

A Open-toad sandals!

Q What is the worst part of the **CLIMBING WALL**?

A The fall!

Q What did the football **COACH** say to the vending machine?

A "I want my quarter-back!"

Q Why is it tough to **COMPETE** against vampires?

A Vampires are always out for blood!

Q What happened after the skiing **COMPETITION** started badly?

A It went downhill fast!

Q What did the archer say when he was almost shot at an archery **CONTEST**?

A "Wow, that was an arrow escape!"

HAHAHA!

15

C

Q Why do **CONTORTIONISTS** make great friends?

A They bend over backward for you!

Q What animal is the star of a **CRICKET** match?

A The bat!

TEE-HEE!

Q How does a **CROSSBOW** archer get in shape?

A Arrow-bics!

Q What happened when the turtle was accidentally hit with a **CROQUET** ball?

A It was shell-shocked!

Q Which soccer players can jump higher than the **CROSSBAR**?

A They all can – crossbars can't jump!

C

Q What do **CROSS-COUNTRY RUNNERS** do when they forget something?

A They try to jog their memories!

Q When is **CROSS-COUNTRY SKIING** easy?

A When you live in a really tiny country!

Q Why did the **CURLING STONE** quit the team?

A It was tired of being pushed around!

HA HA!

Q Why aren't elephants good at **CYCLING**?

A They don't have a thumb to ring the bell!

Q What do **CYCLISTS** do when their handlebars are slippery?

A They get a grip!

Q Did you hear about the clowns that threw **DARTS** into the air?

A They missed!

Q Why did the athlete lose the **DECATHLON**?

A She slipped a discus!

BWAHAHA!

Q Why was the football **DEFENDER** nicknamed "The Archaeologist"?

A Because his career was in ruins!

Q What did the soccer referee say to the chicken who kept tripping **DEFENDERS**?

A "Fowl!"

Q Which dinosaur loves **DEMOLITION DERBY**?

A Tyrannosaurus wrecks, of course!

CACKLE!

Q Why are **DISCUS** throwers talkative?

A They are always discus-ing things!

Q Which **DIVE** have soldiers perfected?

A The cannonball!

Q What kinds of exercises are best for a **DIVER**?

A Pool-ups!

Q Why couldn't the pig take part in the **DIVING** competition?

A Because it pulled a hamstring!

Q How do cattle win games of **DODGEBALL**?

A With good cow-operation!

Q How did the **DOG SLED** team go to college?

A On a collar-ship!

Q What do you call a monkey who wins a medal for **DOWNHILL SKIING**?

A A chimp-ion!

Q Where do sick **DRESSAGE** horses go?

A To the horse-pital!

Q Who hangs upside down in a baseball **DUGOUT**?

A The batboy!

Q Which bird can lift the heaviest **DUMBBELLS**?

A The crane!

HAH!

E

Q Did you hear about the world's worst race **ENTRANT**?

A She ran a bath and came in last!

Q What kind of sandwiches do **EQUESTRIANS** eat?

A Ones made with thorough-bread!

GUFFAW!

Q What **EXERCISES** do hairdressers do at the gym?

A Curls!

Q What are frogs' favorite **EXERCISES**?

A Jumping jacks!

Q How do you organize an **EXTREME SPORTS** tournament in space?

A You planet!

F

Q How do **FEATHERWEIGHT** boxers win fights?

A By tickling their opponents!

Q Why doesn't anyone write jokes about **FENCING**?

A What's the point?

Q Which animals excel at **FIELD HOCKEY**?

A Score-pions!

CHORTLE!

Q Why are **FIGURE SKATERS** blameless?

A They avoid faults!

Q Why was Cinderella so bad at **FIGURE SKATING**?

A Her coach was a pumpkin!

F

Q Which two things stopped the runner from reaching the **FINISH LINE**?

A Her feet!

Q What makes a **FISHERMAN** successful?

A Net profits!

Q Where do gnomes go to get **FIT**?

A Elf spas!

SNICKER!

Q How often do chemists take **FITNESS** classes?

A Only periodically!

Q Why did the two young cows stop playing **FOOTBALL**?

A Because it was calf time!

F

Q What do **FOOTBALL** players drink?

A Penal-tea!

Q What did the manager do when the **FOOTBALL FIELD** was flooded?

A Sent in the subs!

Q What did the tornado say to the **FORMULA ONE** car?

A "Want to go for a spin?"

Q What do you call a **FREESTYLE BMX** with a bed on top?

A Bedridden!

Q Did you hear about the boy who wondered why the **FRISBEE** looked bigger and bigger?

A Finally, it hit him!

LOL!

Q If six elephants get into a car, what **GAME** are they playing?

A Squash!

Q Why do rabbits never see how weekend **GAMES** end?

A Because they're hare today and gone tomorrow!

Q Why did the golfer need new **GLOVES**?

A In case she got a hole-in-one!

HAW-HAW!

Q What is it called when a dinosaur scores a **GOAL**?

A A dino-score!

Q Why were the twin **GOALKEEPERS** upset on their birthday?

A They got red cards!

Q Why did the **GOALPOSTS** get angry?

A Because the bar was rattled!

Q What did the dachshund say when it won a **GOLD MEDAL**?

A "I'm a wiener! I'm a wiener!"

Q What shirt do you wear when you play **GOLF**?

A A tee-shirt!

HE HE!

Q Why is Tarzan such a noisy **GOLFER**?

A He screams every time he swings!

Q How many **GOLFERS** does it take to change a light bulb?

A Fore!

Q Where should **GRAND SLAM** winners live?

A In Tennis-ee!

Q Why did the apple join the **GYM**?

A To work on its core strength!

Q Did you hear about the **GYMKHANA** where the horses were all sad?

A It was a tail of whoa!

Q How long does it take a **GYMNAST** to warm up?

A Just a split second!

Q What happened to the criminals who took up **GYMNASTICS**?

A They ended up behind bars!

SNICKER!

H

Q Why couldn't the dog run in the **HALF MARATHON**?

A It wasn't a part of the human race!

Q Why did a troupe of dancing chickens run onto the field at **HALFTIME**?

A Because the crowd wanted hen-tertainment!

CACKLE!

Q Why was the Egyptian mummy no good at **HANDBALL**?

A It was too wrapped up in itself!

Q How do people who go **HANG GLIDING** for the first time feel afterward?

A Soar all over!

Q How is fighting a **HEAVYWEIGHT BOXER** like doing a crossword puzzle?

A You enter the ring vertical and leave horizontal!

Q What do short **HIGH JUMPERS** do?

A They lower the bar!

Q What should you do on a **HIKE** when you find a fork in the road?

A Stop for lunch!

Q How do **HOCKEY** players kiss?

A They pucker up!

Q What do you call an angry **HOCKEY PLAYER**?

A No more Mr. Ice Guy!

Q What do you call a winged insect that hits **HOME RUNS**?

A A fly swatter!

H

Q When do vampires like **HORSE RACING**?

A When it's neck and neck!

Q What did the **HORSEBACK RIDER** say after being thrown from her horse?

A "Help! I can't giddy-up!"

Q What makes **HOT-AIR BALLOONING** so expensive?

A The cost of inflation!

Q What do **HULA-HOOPERS** say when they get a new hoop?

A "Let's take it out for a spin!"

Q Why were all **HURDLE** events canceled?

A It wasn't a leap year!

BWAHAHA!

Q Why shouldn't you tell jokes on an **ICE RINK**?

A In case the ice cracks up!

Q What is the hardest foot to buy an **ICE SKATE** for?

A A square foot!

Q What do **ICE SKATERS** do when they meet someone new?

A They say something to break the ice!

Q When do **INDY 500** race cars stop working?

A When they are re-tired!

TEE-HEE!

Q How is playing music like **IN-LINE SKATING**?

A If you don't C sharp, you'll B flat!

31

J

Q How is playing the bagpipes like throwing a **JAVELIN** blindfolded?

A You don't have to be very good to get everyone's attention!

Q Why did the **JOCKEY** ride a horse into town?

A Because it was too heavy to carry!

Q What happens if you **JOG** behind a slow-moving car?

A You exhaust yourself!

Q When do **JOGGERS** jog backward?

A When they want to get out of shape!

CHUCKLE!

Q Why was the skeleton afraid to try **JUDO**?

A Because it had no guts!

K

Q Why did the ice cream cone take **KARATE** lessons?

A It was tired of getting licked!

Q Why should you never build a fire while **KAYAKING**?

A Because you can't have your kayak and heat it too!

Q What do you call a pig that learns **KICKBOXING**?

A A pork chop!

Q Why don't **KITE SURFERS** understand kite jokes?

A They go over their heads!

Q Did you hear about the latest **KUNG FU** film?

A It's a real blockbuster and a smash hit!

L

Q Why can't you play **LACROSSE** with pigs?

A They hog the ball!

Q Why did the fish stop **LIFTING** weights?

A It pulled a mussel!

Q What do tired **LINE DANCERS** do?

A They line down!

Q How did the **LONG-DISTANCE RUNNER** run for two hours and only move two feet?

A She only had two feet!

Q What kind of parties do **LUGE** riders go to?

A Snowballs!

GIGGLE!

Q Why are **MARATHON** runners such good students?

A Because they know education pays off in the long run!

Q Which **MARTIAL ART** do vegetarians prefer?

A Kung-tofu!

Q Why can yoga **MASTERS** teach at any time of day?

A Because they are very flexible!

Q When does a British tennis **MATCH** end?

A At Wimble-done!

HA HA!

Q What do cows listen to when learning **MODERN DANCE**?

A Any kind of moo-sic they like!

Q Which **MOTOCROSS** bike is always laughing?

A The Yamaha-ha-ha!

 Why can't **MOTORCYCLES** stand up by themselves?

A Because they are two tired!

Q What's the difference between a scruffy tricycle rider and a well-dressed **MOUNTAIN BIKER**?

A Their at-tire!

Q What do you say to **MOUNTAIN CLIMBERS** when they reach the summit?

A "Hi!"

 Why are **MOUNTAINEERS** always laughing?

A They find everything hill-arious!

CHUCKLE!

Q Why don't **NASCAR** drivers eat before a race?

A In case they get Indy-gestion!

Q Which **NEW ENGLAND PATRIOTS** player wears the biggest helmet?

A The one with the biggest head!

Q What does a **NEW JERSEY NETS** player say when he misses?

A "Shoot!"

Q Why didn't the skeleton play for the **NEW YORK GIANTS**?

A Its heart wasn't in it!

Q Did you hear about the basketball player who got a **NOSEBLEED**?

A It was all over town!

O

Q What's the definition of an **OLYMPIAD**?

A A commercial shown during the Olympic Games!

Q Why couldn't the **OLYMPIANS** listen to music?

A They kept breaking records!

Q What was the banker's favorite **OLYMPIC EVENT**?

A The vault!

Q What's the fastest insect at the **OLYMPIC GAMES**?

A A quicket!

SNICKER!

Q Why did the spotted cat have to hand back its **OLYMPIC MEDAL**?

A Because it was a cheetah!

Q Why were the elephants thrown out of the **OLYMPIC POOL**?

A Because they couldn't keep their trunks up!

Q Who wrote the book about downhill **OLYMPIC SPORTS**?

A Bob Sled!

Q What do **OLYMPIC SPRINTERS** eat before a race?

A Nothing. They fast!

Q Why couldn't the tomato win the race against the lettuce at **OLYMPIC STADIUM**?

A The lettuce was always a-head while the tomato tried to ketchup!

HAH!

Q Who wrote the book ***THE OLYMPIC TRIALS***?

A Willy Qualify!

Q Why were the **PADDLEBOARDERS** so slow?

A Their boards were SUP-side down!

Q Why did the number four refuse to try on the **PARACHUTE**?

A Because it was two squared!

HA HA!

Q What's the hardest part of **PARACHUTING**?

A The ground!

Q How do you make a **PARAGLIDER** pilot do what you want?

A Pull some strings!

Q How do you know that your friends are into **PARKOUR**?

A They're not allowed to set foot in the park!

P

Q Why can't leopards sneak into the **PENALTY AREA**?

A Because they're always spotted!

Q What did the bumblebee say after taking the **PENALTY KICK**?

A "Hive scored!"

HAW-HAW!

Q Why are spiders great **PING-PONG** players?

A Their topspin is ace!

Q What happened when the **POLE VAULTERS** were asked to leave the team?

A They never got over it!

Q What does Cinderella wear on her feet at the swimming **POOL**?

A Glass flippers!

P

Q Why are **POOL PLAYERS** so patient?

A It can take years to get a big break!

Q What do you do with a sick **POWERBOAT**?

A Take it to the doc!

HAHAHA!

Q What did the **POWER WALKERS** say when they walked into the store?

A "Ouch!"

Q What's the difference between a **PRIZEFIGHTER** and a person with a cold?

A One knows their blows, and the other blows their nose!

Q Why do **PRO WRESTLERS** always carry keys?

A So they can get out of hammerlocks!

Q Why did the rider take a **QUAD BIKE** to the doctor?

A It needed a fuel injection!

Q Why did the dog refuse to be a **QUARTERBACK**?

A Because it was a boxer!

Q Who are the **QUICKEST** and most handsome athletes?

A Sprinters – they're always dashing!

Q How do beach volleyball players know when they are playing on **QUICKSAND**?

A They get that sinking feeling!

Q Why did the soccer ball **QUIT** the team?

A It was tired of being kicked around!

HAH!

43

R

Q What happened when two waves had a **RACE**?

A They tide!

SNICKER!

Q What do young **RACEHORSES** use to wrap their food?

A Aluminum foal!

Q What do you get if you cross a **RACING BIKE** with a flower?

A A bike petal!

Q How do **RACE CARS** hear?

A Through their engine-ears!

Q Why are penguins such good **RACING DRIVERS**?

A They're always in pole position!

R

Q How are scrambled eggs like a bad **RACQUETBALL** player?

A They both get beaten!

Q Why are tennis **RACQUETS** so nervous?

A Because they are high-strung!

Q What happened when the red **RAFTING** team crashed into the blue **RAFTING** team?

A They were marooned!

HAW-HAW!

Q What snakes are found on **RALLY CARS**?

A Windshield vipers!

Q What is the best mascot for a **RELAY TEAM**?

A A lapdog!

R

Q Why do **RHYTHMIC GYMNASTS** add salt to their food when the sun shines?

A Because they love summer salts!

Q What do you call a boxer who has just received a strong **RIGHT HOOK**?

A A sore loser!

Q What can help shy people with **ROCK CLIMBING**?

A Getting a bit boulder!

Q What kind of dinosaur loves **RODEO RIDING**?

A A bronco-saurus!

Q What would you call a bird's **ROLLERBLADES**?

A Cheep skates!

CHUCKLE!

R

Q Why did the **ROLLER SKATERS** skate all the way to Egypt?

A They needed to visit the Cairo-practor!

Q Who wrote the boxing book *Out in the First* **ROUND**?

A Major Disaster!

Q Where does the ghost **ROWING** team practice?

A Lake Eerie!

HE HE!

Q Why are **RUGBY** players so determined?

A They are always willing to give it one last try!

Q What did the **RUGBY BALL** say to the shoe?

A "I get a kick out of you!"

R

Q Why did the **RUGBY PLAYER** go to see the vet?

A Because her calves were hurting!

Q What can **RUN** but can't walk?

A A drop of water!

SNICKER!

Q What is a **RUNNER'S** favorite subject?

A Jog-raphy!

Q Why did the bald man take up **RUNNING**?

A He wanted to get some fresh hair!

Q What do you call **RUNNING SHOES** made from bananas?

A Slippers!

S

Q What's the worst vegetable to serve on a **SAILBOAT**?

A Leeks!

Q Why did the opera singers go **SAILING**?

A Because they wanted to hit the high Cs!

Q Which member of a **SAILING CREW** blows their nose a lot?

A The anchor-chief!

Q How do **SCUBA DIVERS** bathe?

A They wash up on shore!

HAW-HAW!

Q What can you **SERVE** but not eat?

A A tennis ball!

Q What's a **SHOT-PUTTER'S** favorite airport in England?

A Heathrow!

Q What happened when Minton the dog ate two **SHUTTLECOCKS**?

A Its owner said, "Bad Minton, bad Minton!"

Q Why are **SIT-UPS** the easiest kinds of exercise?

A Because they include the most lying down!

Q Why won't the **SKATEBOARDER** tell his dad about his dangerous new trick?

A He thinks heel flip!

HA HA!

Q What do you get when you cross a **SKIER** and a vampire?

A Frostbite!

S

Q What shouldn't a **SKYDIVER** ever do?

A Jump to conclusions!

LOL!

Q How is a **SKYDIVING SCHOOL** unlike any other school?

A You have to drop out to graduate!

Q Why are actors so good at playing **SNOOKER**?

A They know their cues!

Q Where do **SNOWBOARDERS** keep their money?

A In a snowbank!

Q What's the difference between a dog and a **SOCCER PLAYER**?

A One drools while the other dribbles!

S

Q Why did the **SOCCER TEAM** spin their trophy around and around?

A Because it was the Whirled Cup!

CHORTLE!

Q How is a **SOFTBALL** team similar to pancakes?

A They both need good batters!

Q Did you hear about the **SPEED SKATER** who broke her elbow?

A It was really humerus!

Q What's a horse's favorite **SPORT**?

A Stable tennis!

Q What happened to the **SPORTSPEOPLE** whose shoes were too small?

A They suffered the agony of defeat!

S

Q How do you start a firefly **SPRINT** race?

A "Get ready, get set, glow!"

Q Why are waiters so good at **SQUASH**?

A Because they are excellent servers!

Q Why are sports **STADIUMS** cool?

A Because they are full of fans!

HAHAHA!

Q Did you hear about the one-legged **SUMO WRESTLER**?

A He was a total pushover!

Q How do **SURFERS** greet each other?

A They wave!

53

Q What do hungry **SWIMMERS** spread on their toast?

A Butter-fly!

Q Where do zombies go **SWIMMING**?

A In the Dead Sea!

Q Why did the teachers jump into the **SWIMMING POOL**?

A Because they wanted to test the waters!

Q Which **SWIMMING STROKE** do babies like best?

A The crawl!

Q When is your **SWIMSUIT** like a bell?

A When you wring it out!

CACKLE!

Q What do a dentist and a **TABLE TENNIS** coach have in common?

A They both use drills!

Q Why did the **TAE KWON DO** master wear a black belt?

A To keep her pants up!

Q How did the tailor feel when his favorite **TEAM** tied the game?

A Sew-sew!

Q Why didn't the **TENNIS** player get married?

A Because in tennis love means nothing!

TEE-HEE!

Q Why do **TENNIS INSTRUCTORS** love vending machines?

A Because they don't have to wait for their food to be served!

Q Why were the **TIGHTROPE** walkers disqualified?

A Because they didn't stick to the straight and narrow!

HAH!

Q Why was the barber disqualified from the **TOUR DE FRANCE**?

A Because of a shortcut!

Q Which tennis **TOURNAMENT** never closes?

A The US Open!

Q What direction do chickens run around the **TRACK**?

A Cluck-wise!

Q What time of year is best for **TRAMPOLINING**?

A Spring time!

Q What do **TRAMPOLINISTS** do when they get sick?

A Try to bounce back!

Q Why was the **TRAPEZIST** worried?

A Because everything was up in the air!

Q Why is running on a **TREADMILL** pointless?

A Because it gets you nowhere fast!

Q What do you say to King Kong when he wins the **TRIPLE JUMP**?

A "Kong-ratulations!"

GUFFAW!

Q What do you call a group of pigs playing **TUG-OF-WAR**?

A Pulled pork!

U

Q What's the difference between a baseball **UMPIRE** and an empire?

A An umpire gives three strikes, but an *Empire Strikes Back*!

Q Why do **UNICYCLISTS** only eat one small chunk of chocolate at a time?

A Because they can't handle-bars!

BWAHAHA!

Q Where do soccer players go to get new **UNIFORMS**?

A New Jersey!

Q When do boxers look forward to receiving an **UPPERCUT**?

A When they're at the salon!

Q What time do **US OPEN** tennis players go to bed?

A Ten-nish!

CACKLE!

Q Why should you consider taking up the pole **VAULT**?

A It can jump-start your career!

Q Did you hear about the **VELODROME** for vampires?

A It was a vicious cycle!

Q Did you hear about the **VOLLEYBALL** that was arrested?

A It's waiting to go to court!

Q Why did the **VOLLEYBALL COACH** take string onto the court?

A To tie the score!

Q What does a carpenter have in common with a **VOLLEYBALL PLAYER**?

A They both like to hammer spikes!

Q What happened when the comedians tried **WATER POLO**?

A Their horses sank!

Q How do you stop squirrels from **WATERSKIING** in your backyard pond?

A Hide their skis, it drives them nuts!

Q What kind of vegetable likes **WEIGHT TRAINING**?

A A muscle sprout!

Q What's the best day for **WINDSURFING**?

A Winds-day!

Q What do the **WINNERS** of a race lose?

A Their breath!

CHUCKLE!

Q Did you hear about the 120-year-old soccer players at the **WORLD CUP**?

A They were still alive and kicking!

Q Who wrote the book *How to Beat a* **WORLD RECORD**?

A Vic Tory!

Q How does a **WRESTLER** buy soda?

A In six packs!

Q Why did the sausage quit **WRESTLING**?

A It was the wurst on the team!

HAW-HAW!

Q What did the catcher say when she saw an **X-RAY** of her broken finger?

A "On the other hand, I'm perfectly fine!"

Q Why couldn't the crew play cards on the **YACHT**?

A Because the captain was standing on the deck!

Q Why did the **YACHTING** team pull out of the race?

A Pier pressure!

Q Why was the chicken shown a **YELLOW CARD**?

A For fowl play!

Q What's the most romantic kind of **YOGA POSITION**?

A The pro-pose!

Q What kind of animal makes a good **YOGA TEACHER**?

A A Shangri-llama!

Q What happens in a **ZINC** swimming pool?

A The swimmers either zinc or swim!

Q Why are **ZIP LINES** disappointing?

A They're always a letdown!

Q What's the problem with **ZIP-LINING** events?

A All the hanging around!

Q What happened when the **ZORB FOOTBALL** team kept losing?

A They just rolled with it!

Q Why did the newlyweds go **ZORBING**?

A They were head over heels in love!

GUFFAW!

LOL!

CACKLE!

HE HE!

HA HA!

BWAHAHA!

First American Edition 2020
Kane Miller, A Division of EDC Publishing
Copyright © Green Android Ltd 2019
Illustrated by Vasco Icuza

For information contact:
Kane Miller, A Division of EDC Publishing
P.O. Box 470663
Tulsa, OK 74147-0663
www.kanemiller.com
www.edcpub.com
www.usbornebooksandmore.com

Library of Congress Control Number: 2019936213

Printed and bound in Malaysia, November 2019
ISBN: 978-1-61067-999-2